For a ▬ ▬

at

Enjoy!

—Shaun Vain

(Future Publishing House)

GRIFFIN'S FIRST DAY OF SCHOOL

Written by Jason Ruby
Illustrated by Tony Lopez

Future
Publishing House
KID LIT

This book is dedicated to my son Griffin

The inspiration for my book was my son who is named Griffin.

After he was born, I was shocked at how hard it was to find griffin toys and books about griffins. I thought they would have been as popular as dragons. After all griffins show up on medieval crests, in many different lores around the world, and in a large array of video games, but I was wrong. For children stories and young readers, they are a considerably tough creature to find.

So one day, I was sitting at home watching tv and I had an idea. What if all mythical creatures went to school? I grabbed a marble notebook and started outlining an idea. Before the night was done, I had a nice outline and a plethora of characters to put in this book. I did want to make sure the creatures are from different regions and historical time periods to keep the story fresh and fun. I hope you enjoy and thanks for reading.

Special thanks to Katie B, Mia C, Lys S, Andrew C, Erin L, Erin R, and Tony L for all your help in making this project a reality.

Today is Griffin's first day of school. He waves goodbye to his dad and heads up the stairs to school with his friend Pegasus.

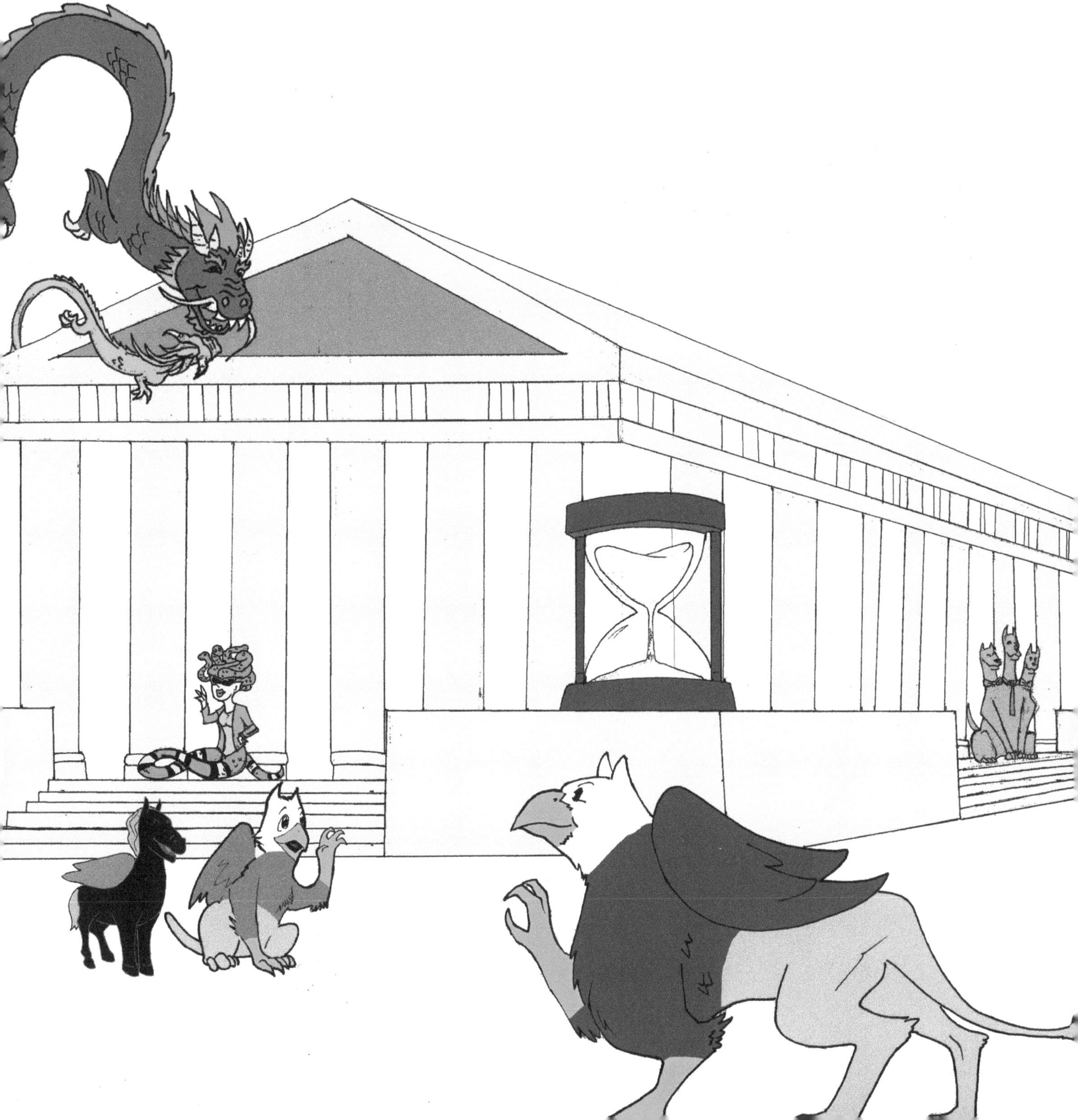

School is much different than anything Griffin has experienced. The hallways are packed with creatures of all ages and types.

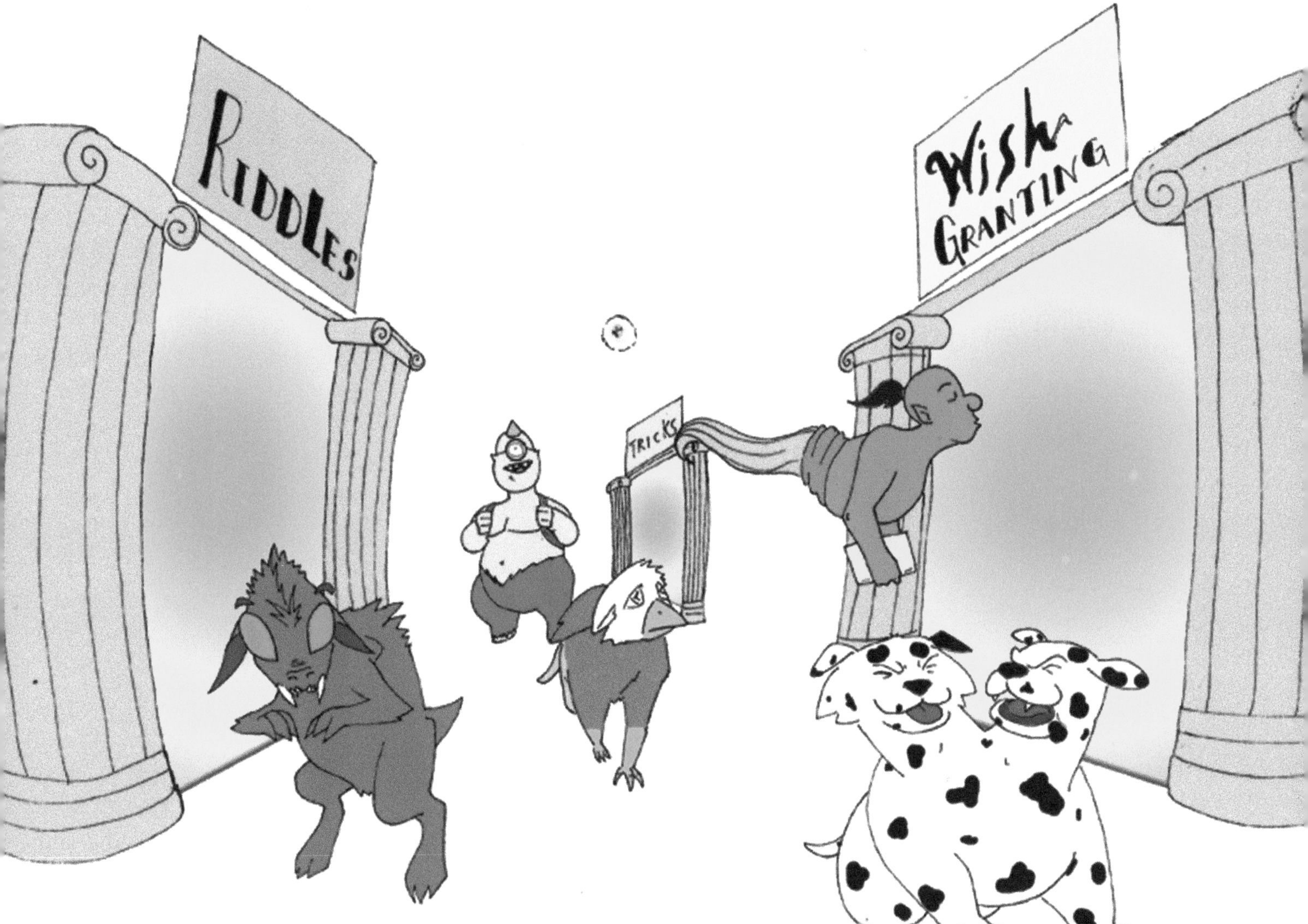

RIDDLES
WISH GRANTING
TRICKS

Math is Griffin's first class. Griffin's teacher is Mr. Hydra, who has five heads! One head of Mr. Hydra is teaching addition, while another head explains how he has enough eyes to keep track of everyone in class. Griffin finds math boring and hopes his next class will be more fun.

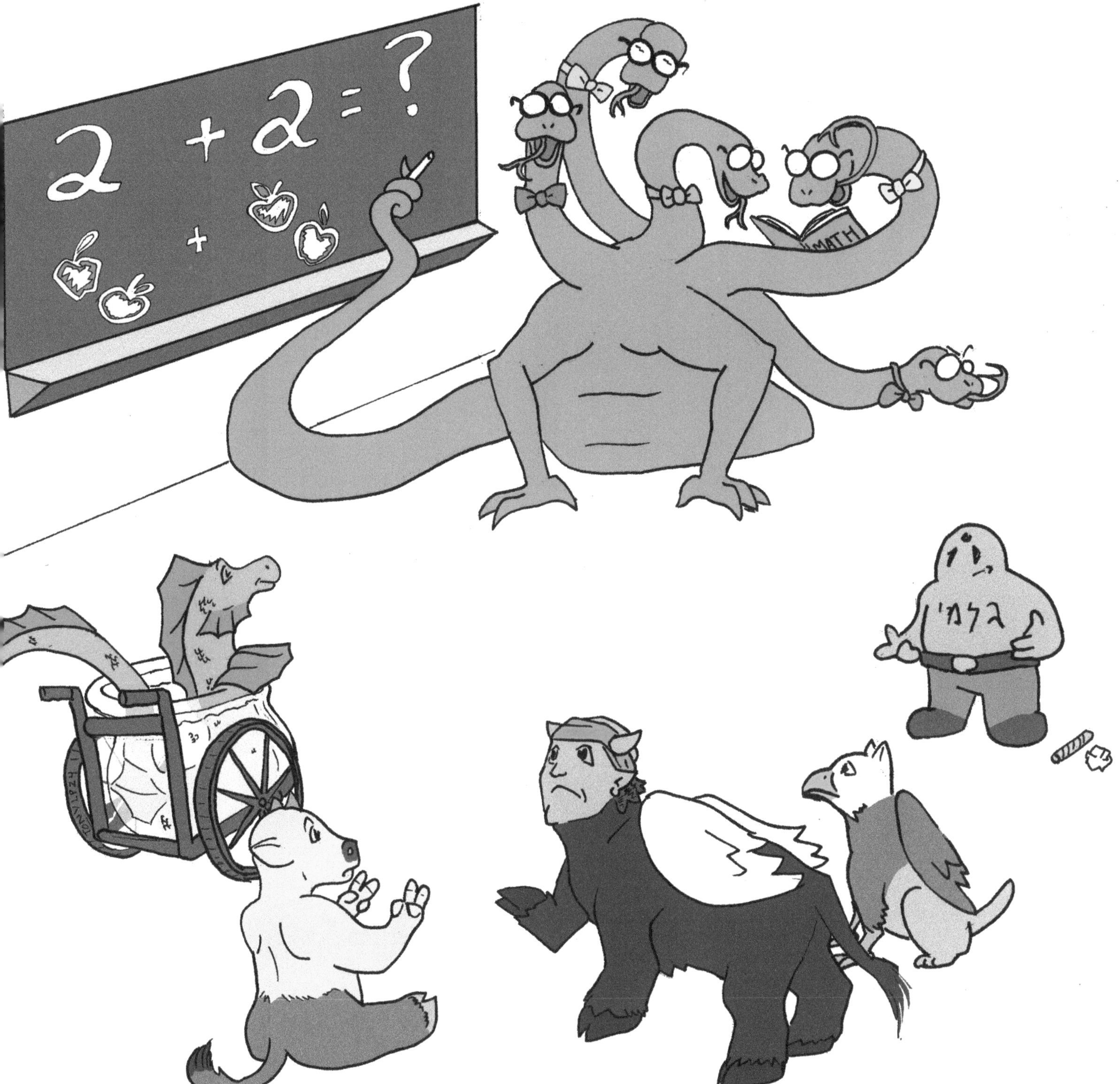
2 + 2 = ?
+
MATH
גלמי

Griffin's next class is Treasure Guarding. His teacher, Mr. Leprechaun, explains the lesson, "Today, we will work on being scary!" Griffin is very nervous because he doesn't know how to be scary.

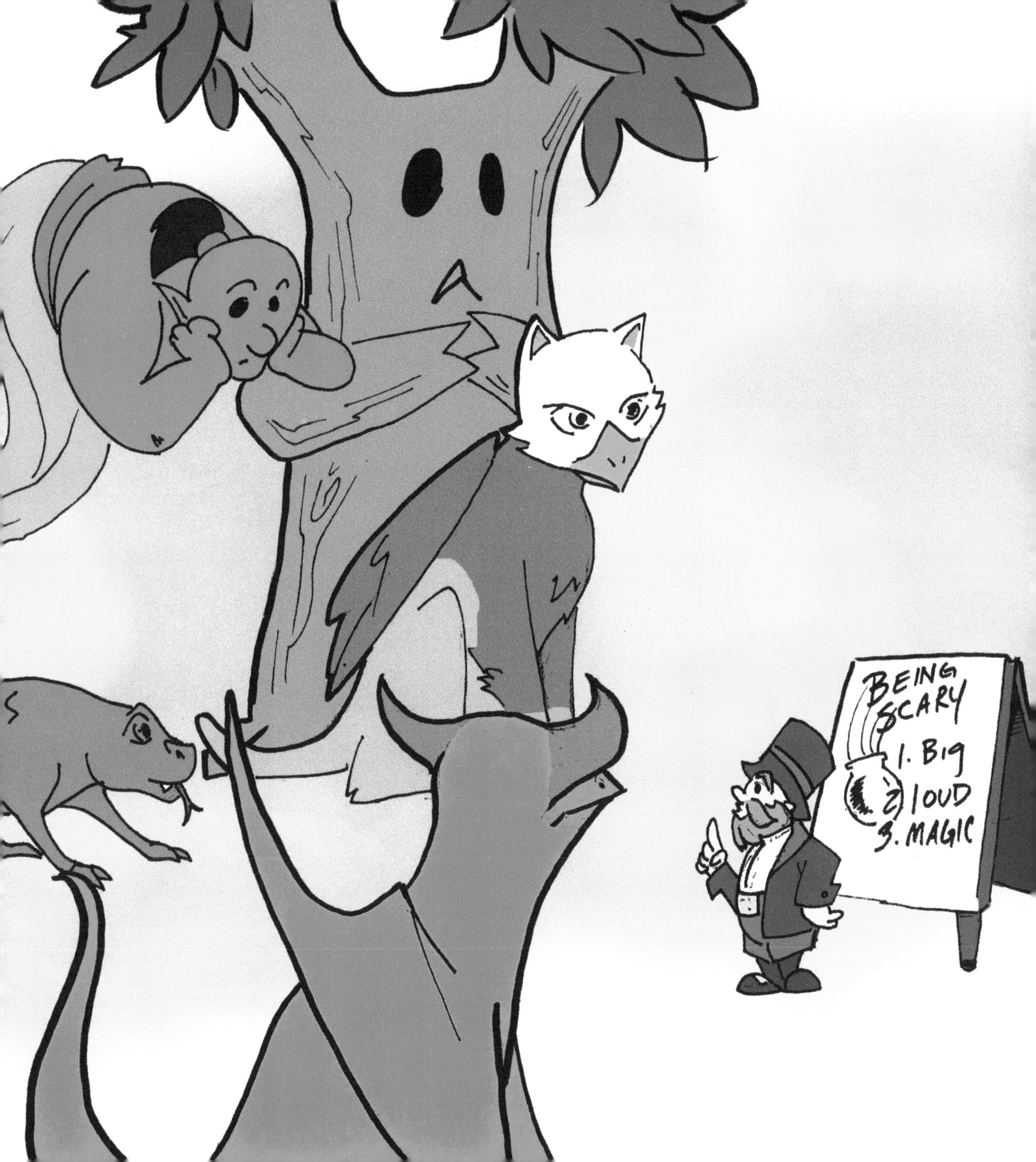
BEING SCARY
1. Big
2. lOUD
3. MAGIC

All the other creatures go before Griffin.

Dragon opens her wings and ROARS!

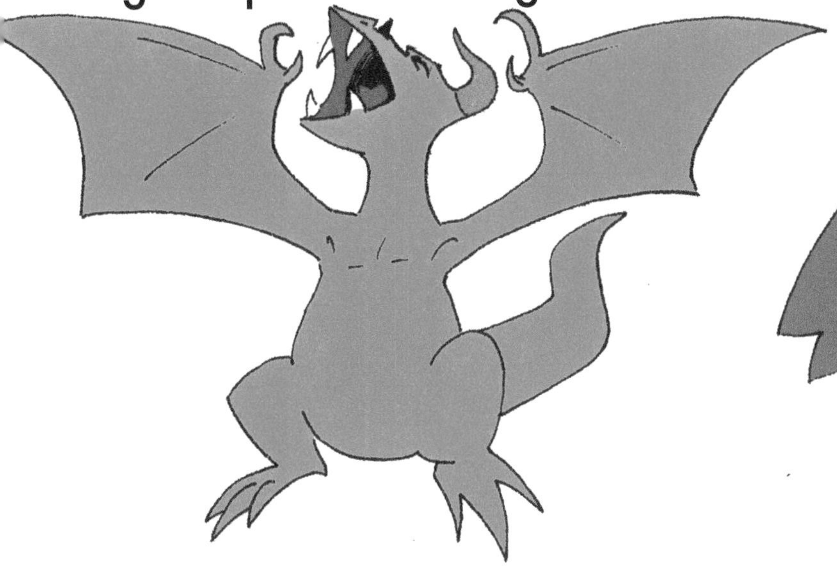

Spriggon grows taller and screams, "AHHH!"

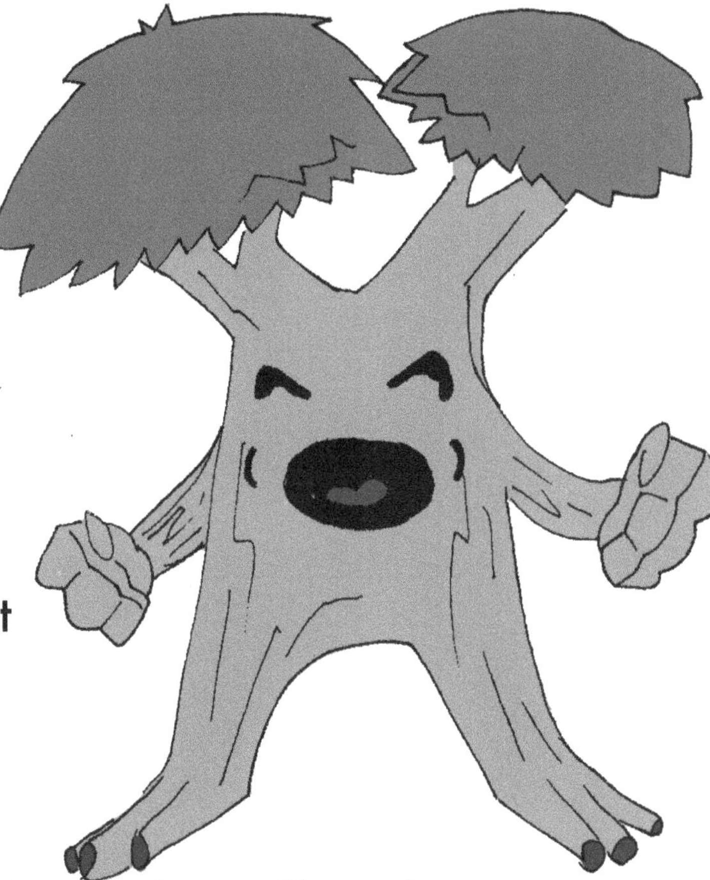

Jinn's eyes turn to fire and he lets out an eerie laugh, "HEHEHEHEHEHE!"

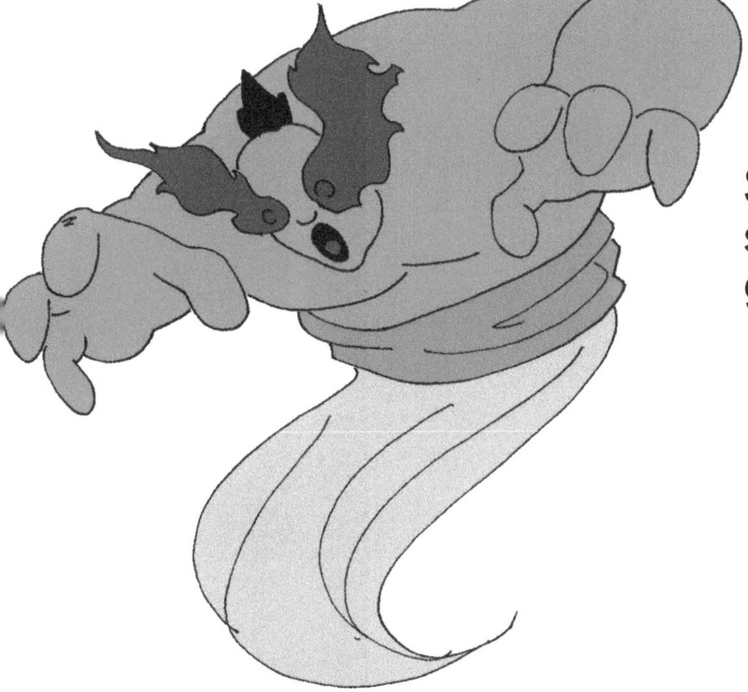

Salamander puffs up big, surrounds herself with fire and growls, "GRR!"

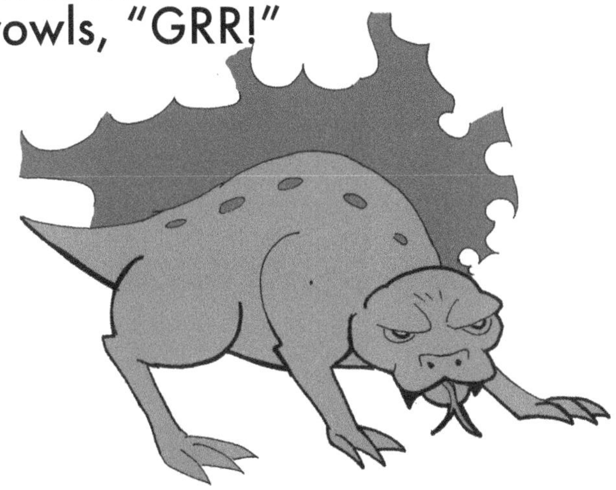

But when it's Griffin's turn to be scary, all he can manage is a tiny squeak.

All the other students laugh. Dragon yells, "You're not scary! We are going to call you Squeaky from now on!"

Griffin is so embarrassed. He just wants school to be over.

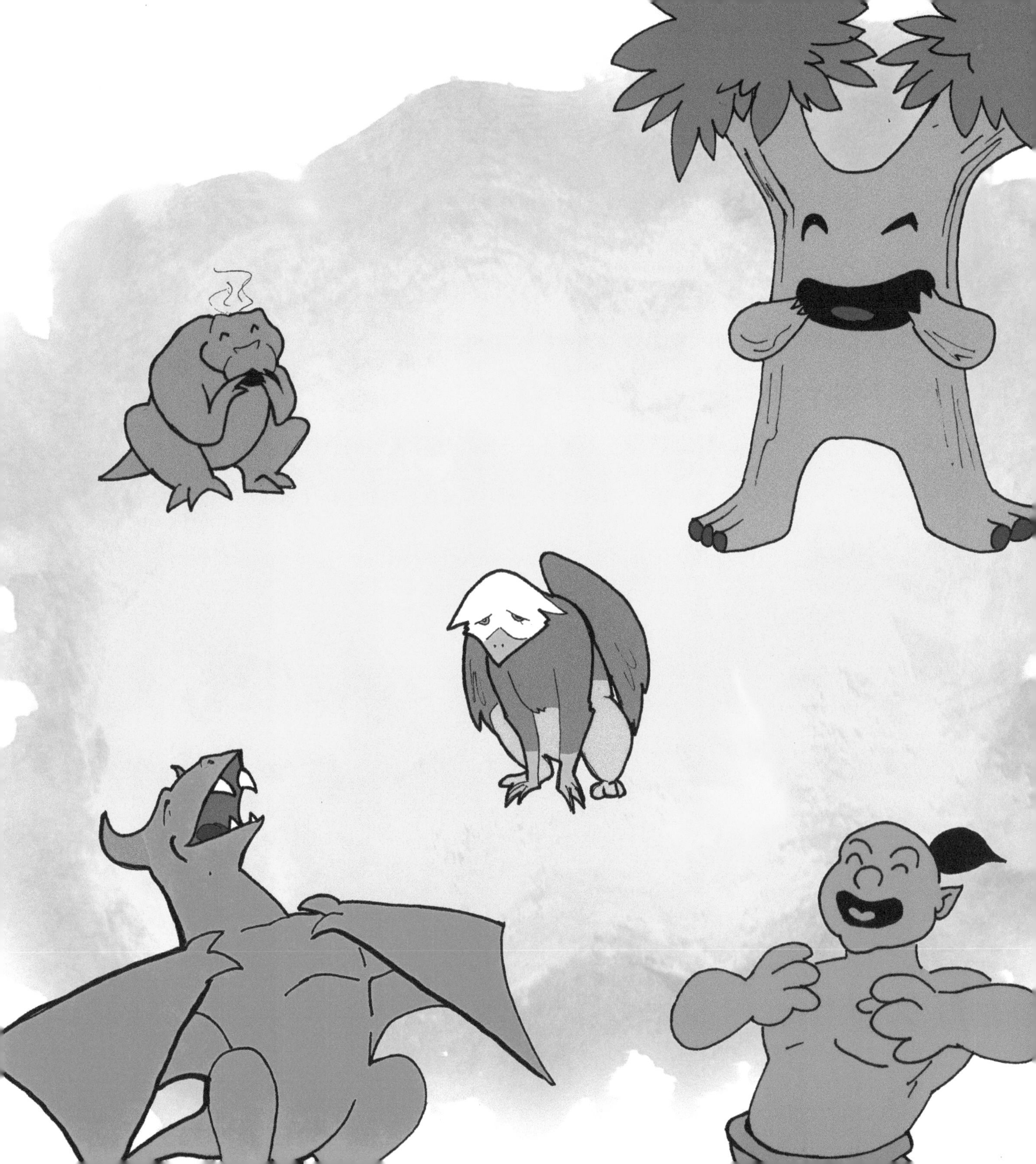

Lunch is next. Griffin is happy to have a break from class! He tells his best friend, Pegasus, what happened and how he wishes the day was over. Pegasus tries to cheer up Griffin and tells him that he had a hard time in his Hero Carrying class, too.

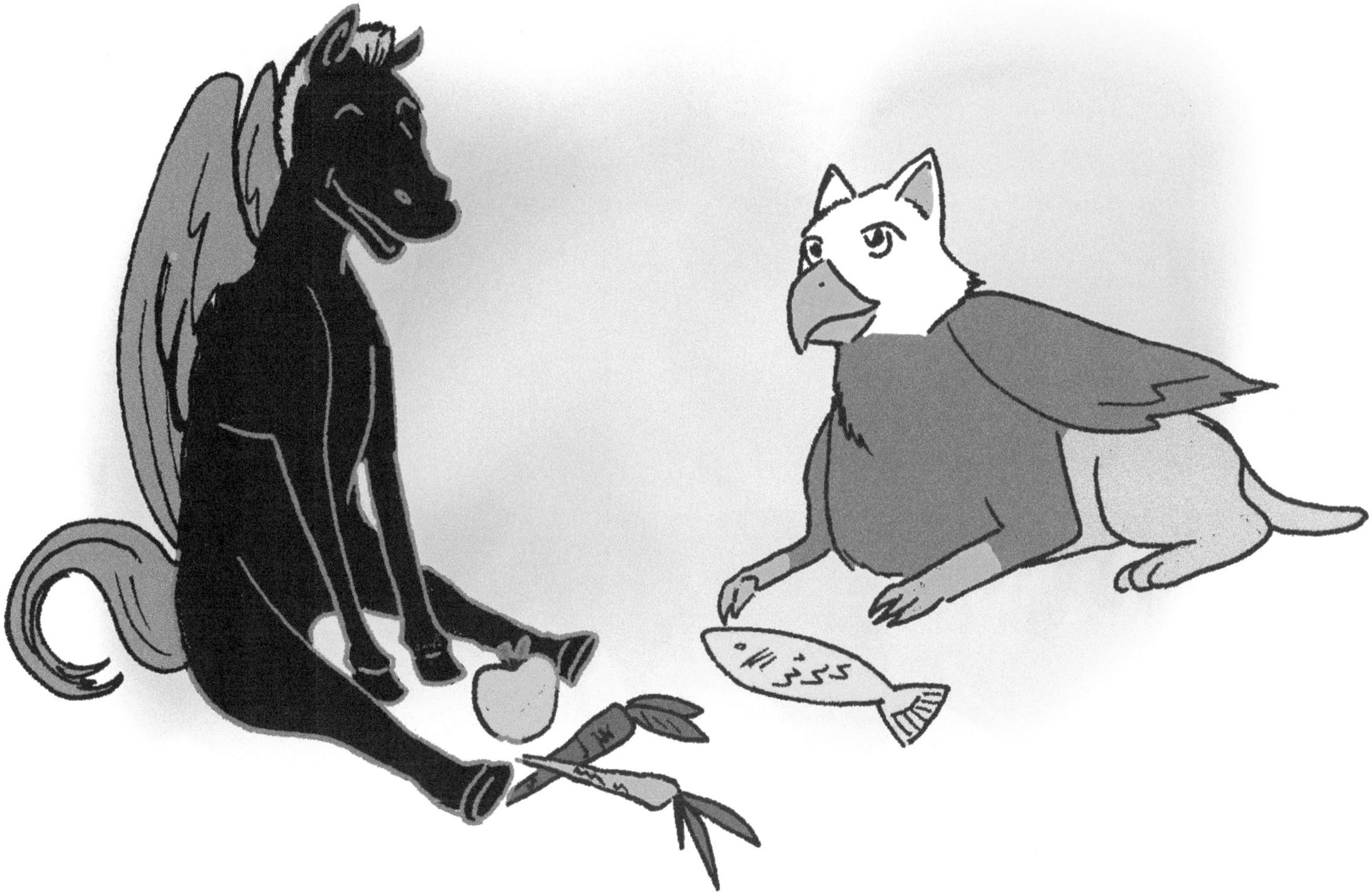

After lunch, Griffin has Hunting class. All the creatures pounce on slippery balls.

The teacher is explaining to Ogre, "I said pounce, not pound." Ogre responds: "Sorry, Ms. Clary."

Griffin has lots of fun and forgets all about Treasure Guarding class.

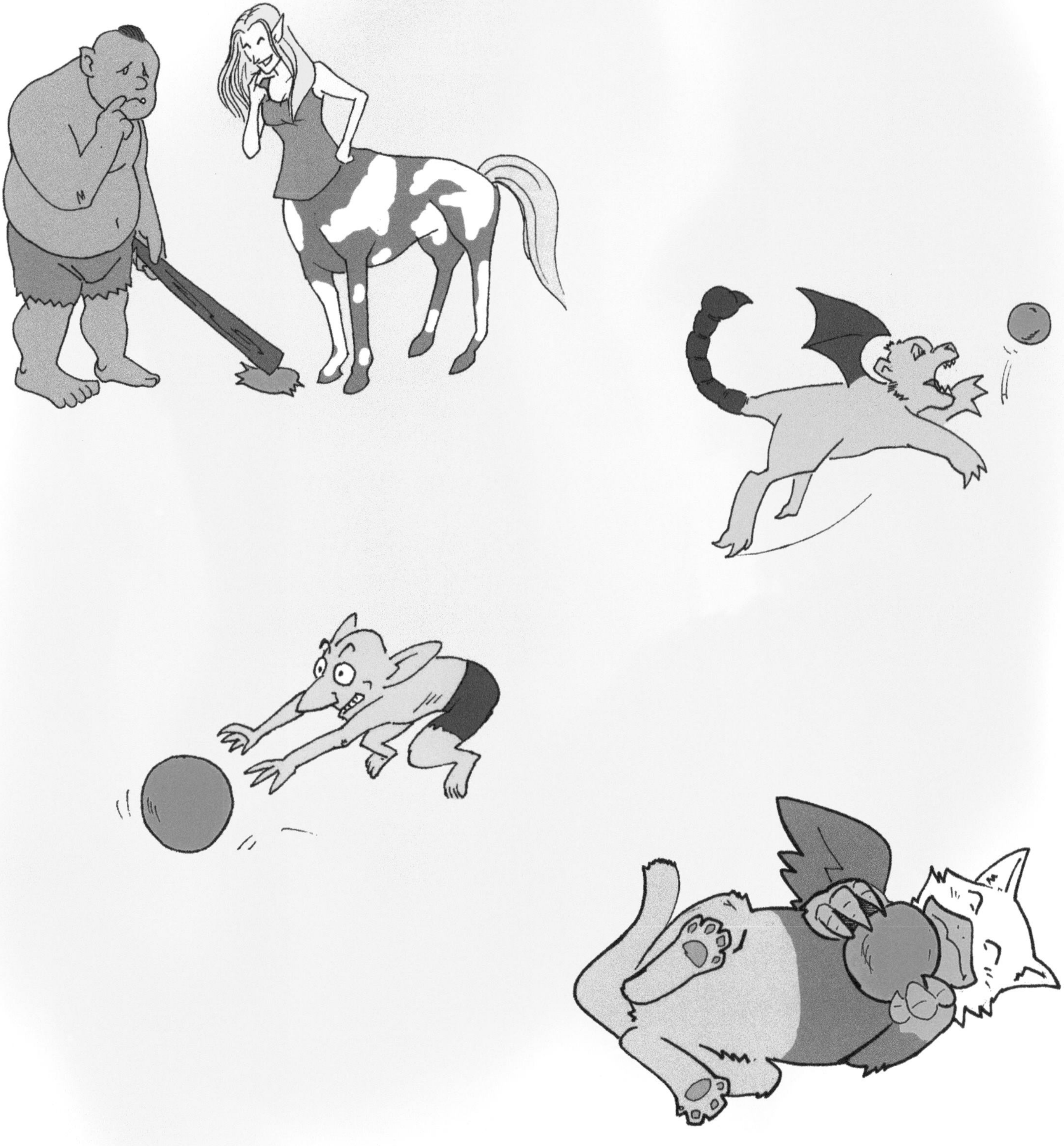

Griffin's last class of the day is Flying. Griffin is happy to see his friend Pegasus but is nervous because Dragon is also in the class.

Griffin's teacher, Mr. Phoenix, explains the day's lesson. "Today, we learn the basics of taking off. All I want you to do is run down this path and, after a couple of steps, start flapping your wings."

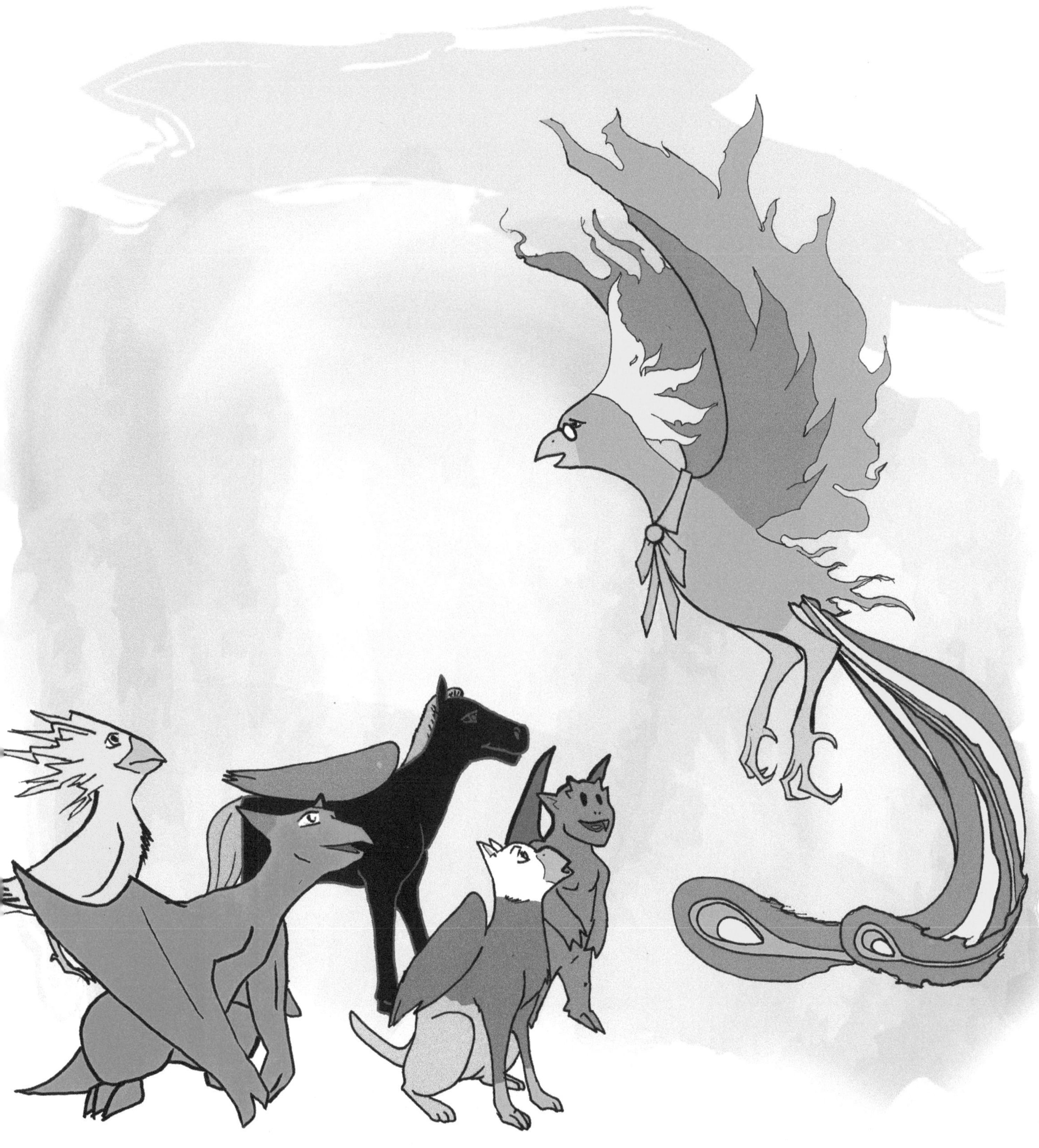

Pegasus goes first. He makes it look easy.

It's Griffin's turn next. He is scared that he will be laughed at again. Griffin takes a deep breath and starts to run. Then, he closes his eyes and starts to flap his wings.

He hears Pegasus yell, "OPEN YOUR EYES!"

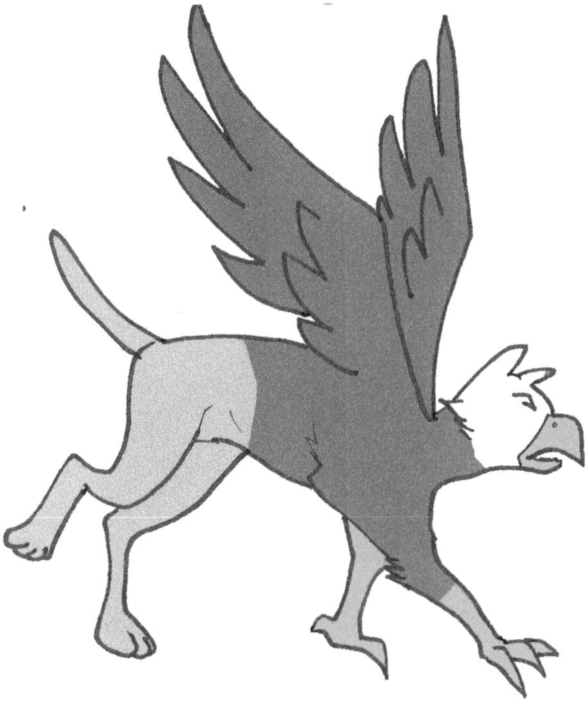

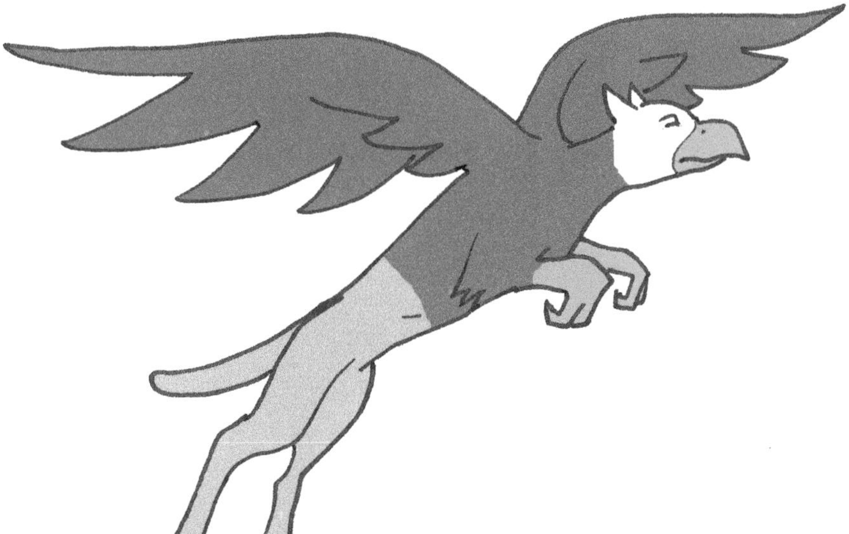

Griffin opens his eyes and discovers he is flying! His classmates are all very excited for him.

Pegasus, Thunder Bird and Gargoyle are all cheering for Griffin. Meanwhile, Dragon is showing how unimpressed she is by rolling her eyes and saying, "So what, I can do better."

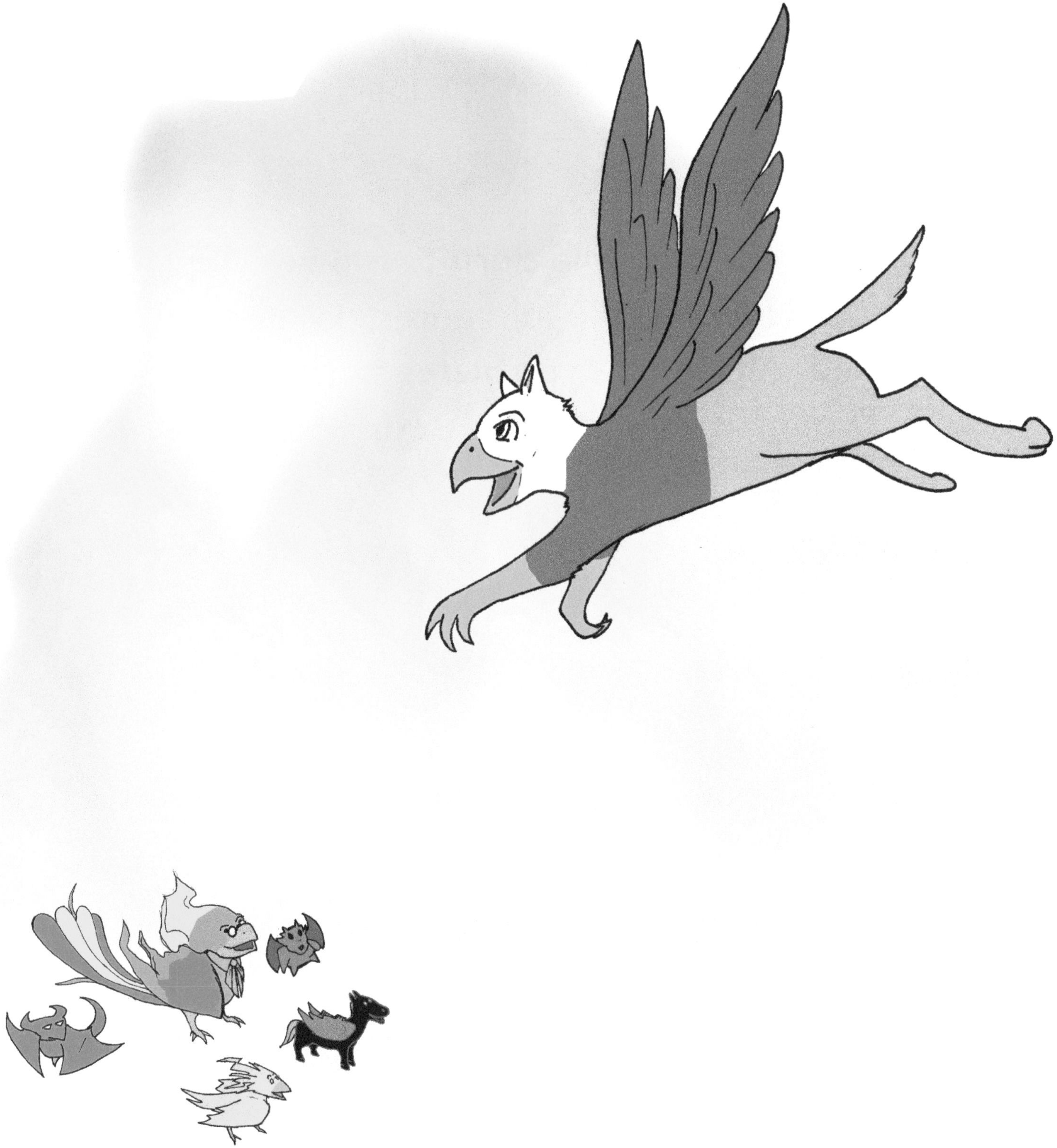

Dragon's turn is next. She starts to run and flap her wings. Suddenly, she falls and slides across the ground. All the other creatures start to laugh. Dragon is very embarrassed.

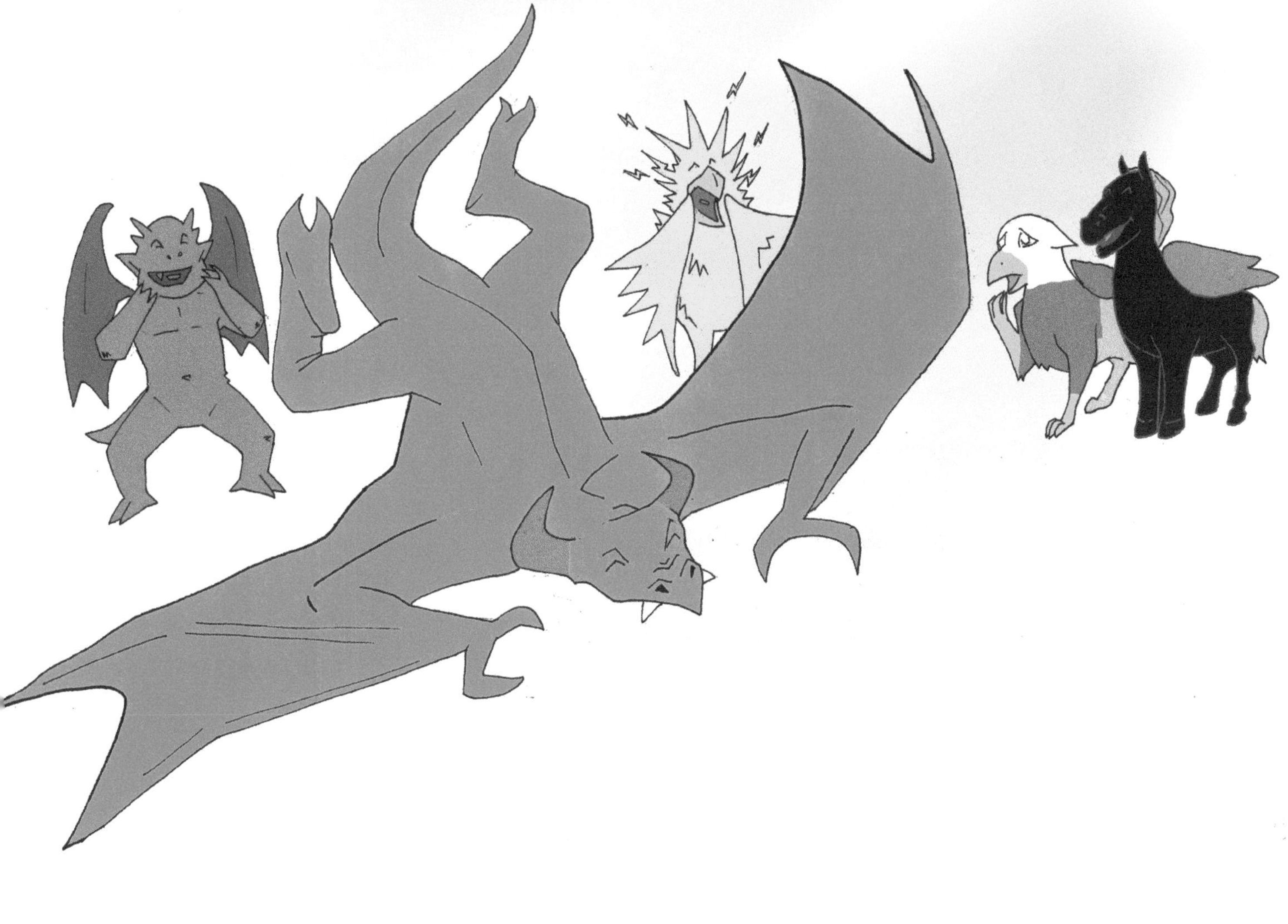

Griffin understands what it is like to be laughed at and decides to speak up for Dragon instead of making fun of her.

Griffin stands between Dragon and his other classmates. He says, "It's not nice to laugh at someone just because they made a mistake. It's just the first day. We will all get better."

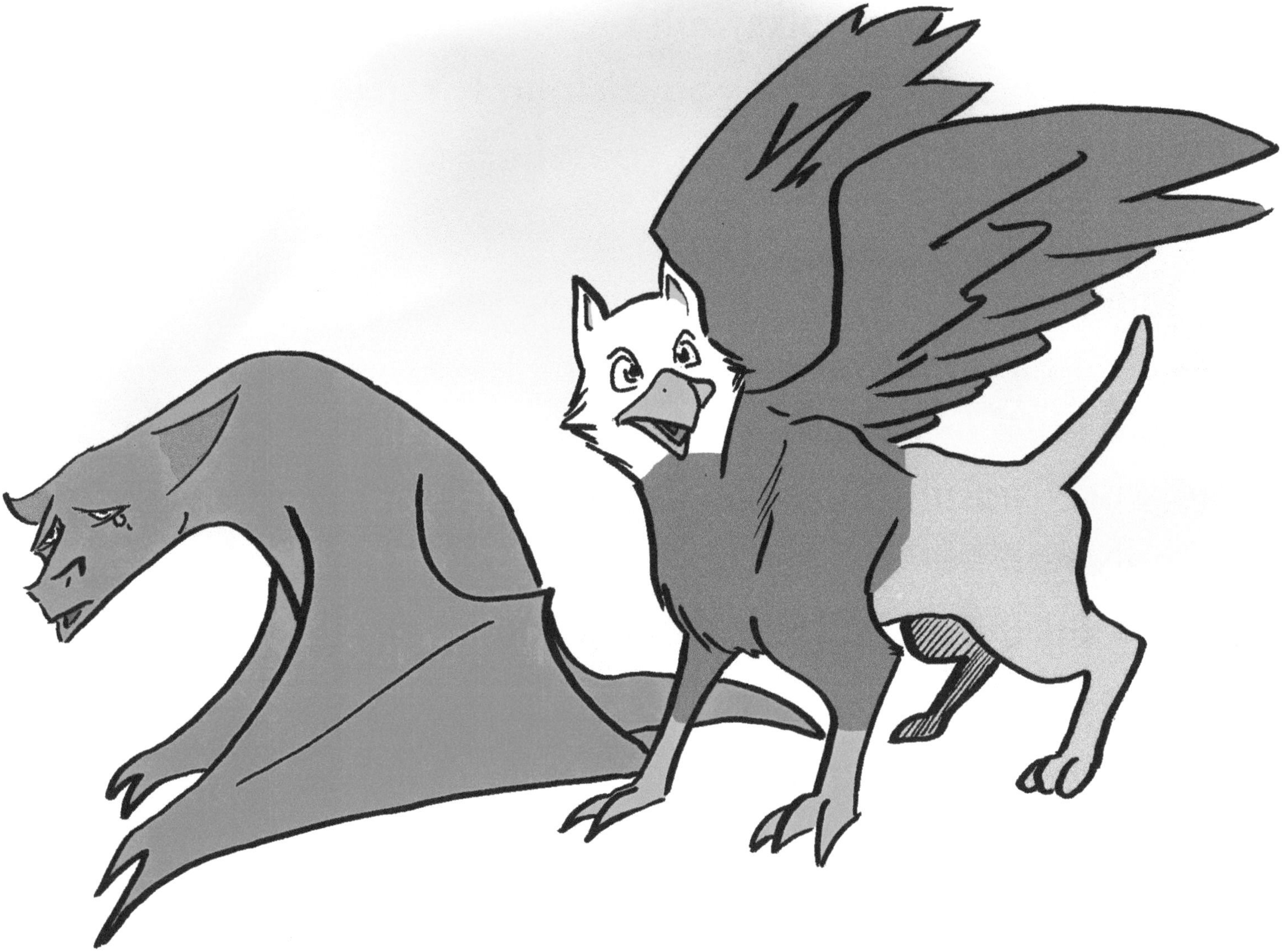

After class Dragon talks with Griffin.
Dragon asks, "Why did you stick up for me?
I was mean and laughed at you after you
made a mistake."

Griffin responds by saying, "I know what it's
like to be laughed at and don't think anyone
should have to experience that. If you help
me with Treasure Guarding, I can help you
with flying."

Dragon is excited and says, "I think that is a
great idea!"

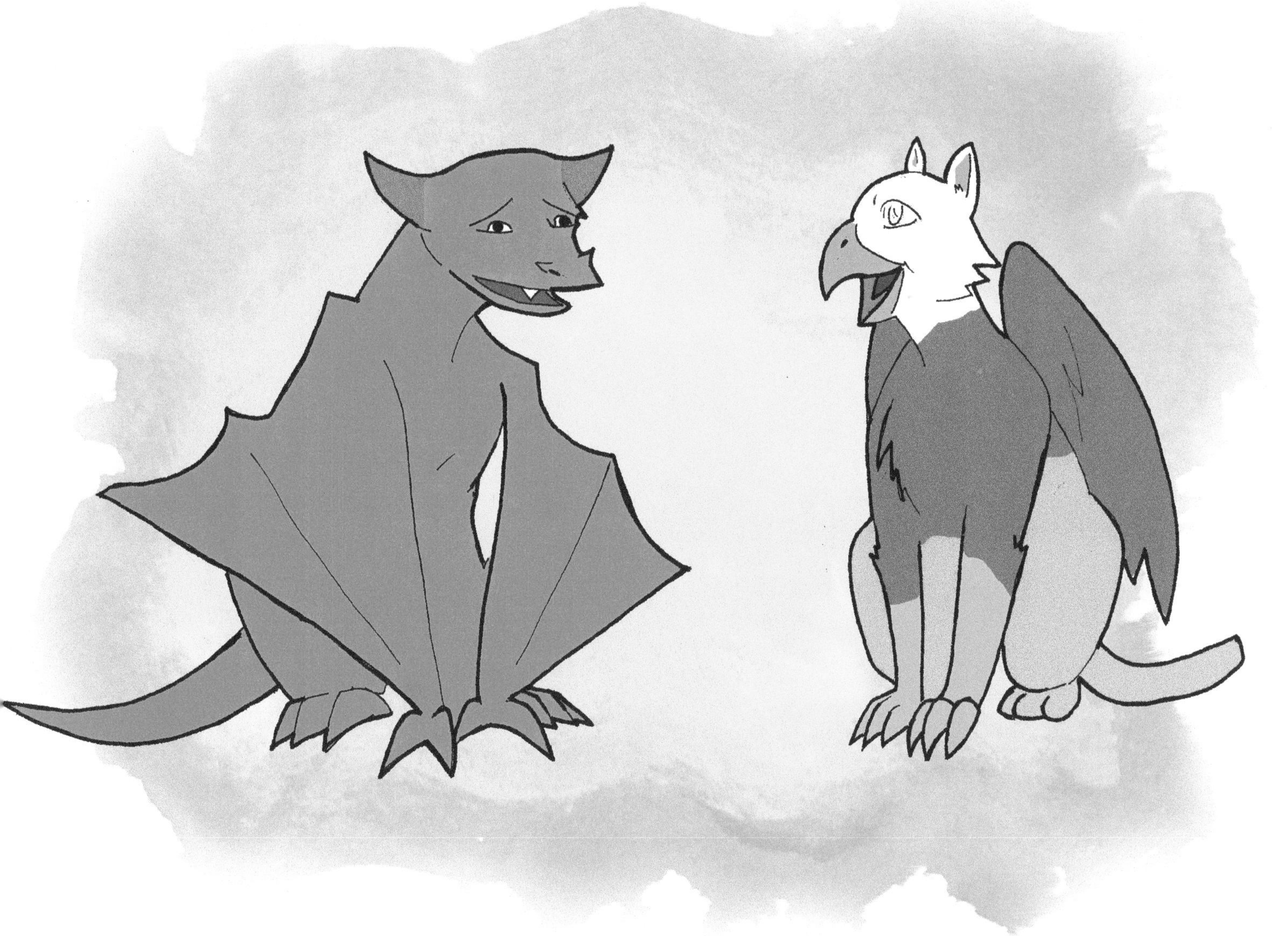

Griffin made a new friend today, and all the friends leave their first day of school, excited for what they will learn the next day.

Griffin, Pegasus and Dragon all walk down the steps together and say, "See you tomorrow!"

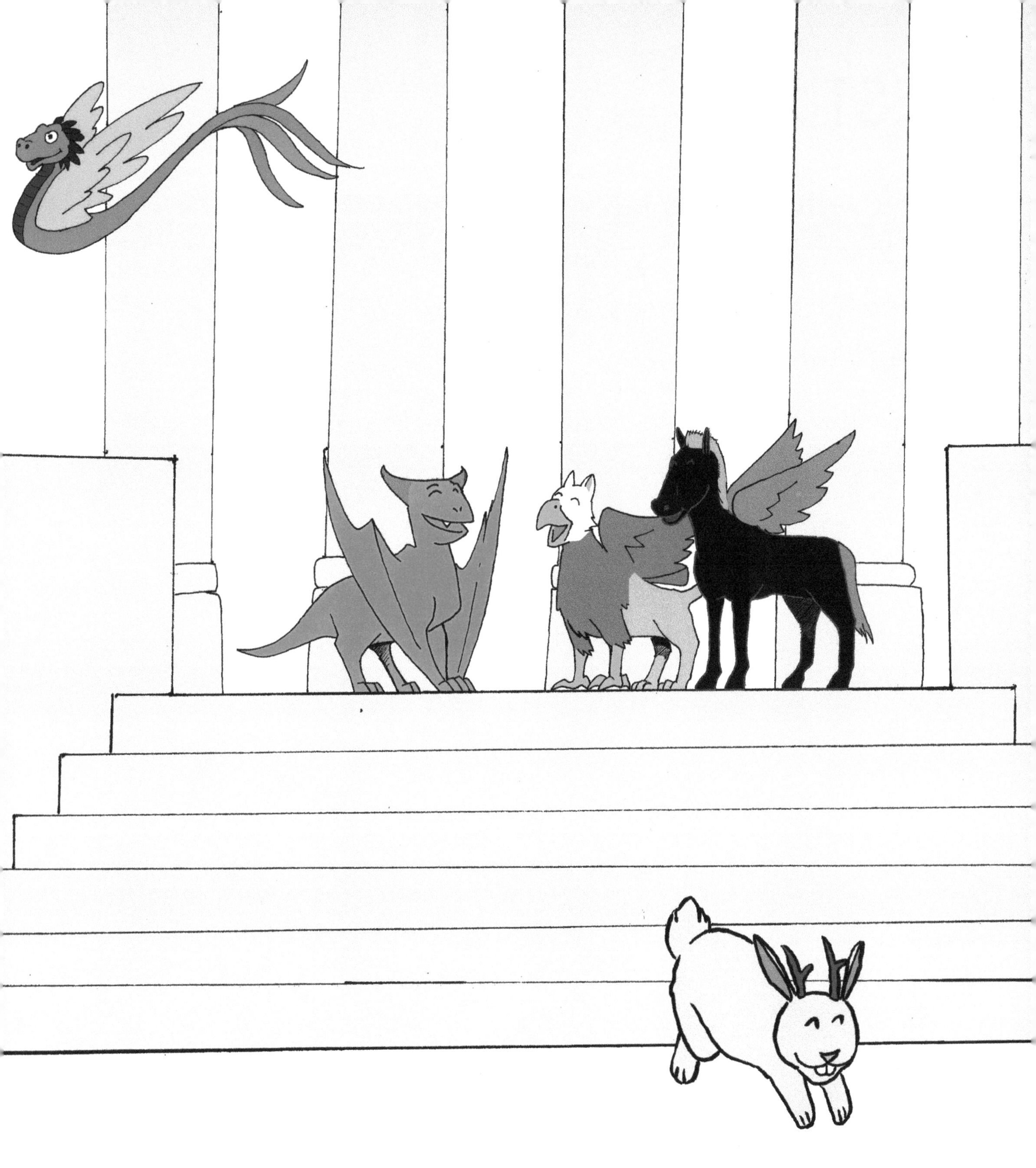

BESTIARY

If you would like to learn more about the creatures in this story, please read on. When it comes to appearances, some creative licenses were taken.

Centauride: Greek

Female centaurs are called centaurides. They are creatures with the upper body of a human and the lower body and legs of a horse. Centaurs and centaurides are excellent hunters and warriors.

Cerberus: Greek/Roman

Cerberus is a multi-headed dog that guards the gates of the Underworld to prevent the dead from leaving. The three heads represent past, present and future.

Chupacabra: North/South American

The chupacabra is a creature from the Americas, including Mexico, Puerto Rico and the United States. It is known to pester farmers by eating their livestock. Its name means "Goat Sucker."

Cyclopes: Greek/Roman

Cyclopes are giant one-eyed humanoid creatures with enormous strength. They are also said to be great blacksmiths and creators of thunderbolts.

Eastern dragon: East Asian

Eastern dragons have many animal-like forms such as turtles and fish, but they are most commonly depicted as snake-like with four legs and do not have wings like their European cousins. The number of claws on a dragon's talon determines its strength and wisdom.

European dragons: European

European dragons are depicted as large, winged reptilian creatures with horns and four legs. They are capable of breathing fire, ice or poison. They are believed to inhabit caves, mountains and abandoned castles, where they guard their vast hordes of treasure.

Gargoyles: European

Gargoyles are creatures made of granite, basalt, or another type of strong stone. They often roost on churches, castles, and other large structures. Their growls and frightening expressions are used to scare away evil spirits

Goblins: European

Goblins are mischievous creatures with magical abilities. They are almost always small with a long nose and bat-like ears. They are greedy and love gold and jewelry.

Golem: Jewish

Golems are animated creatures that are created from inanimate matter, such as stone, clay or mud. Golems are used as helpers, companions or rescuers of endangered Jewish communities.

Griffin: Persian/European/Eastern Asian/Christian

The griffin is a large, legendary creature with the body, tail and back legs of a lion, and the head, wings and front feet of an eagle. They are believed to guard gold mines and treasure caches. Griffins symbolize power and wisdom.

Hippocampus: Etruscan/Pictish/Roman/Greek

The hippocampus is depicted as having the upper body of a horse with the lower body of a fish. Poseidon, God of the Sea, is said to ride a chariot pulled by a pair of hippocampi.

Hydra: Greek/Roman

The hydra has many heads. If you cut off one hydra head, two more grow back in its place. The middle head of the hydra can breathe fire, and the other heads are able to breathe poison.

Jackalope: North American

The jackalope is described as a jackrabbit with antelope horns. Jackalopes have a great singing voice and have been known to sing along at night while people are singing around the campfire.

Jinn: Arabian/Islamic

Jinn or genies are creatures of fire or wind. They can take on any form they choose. They have been known to be imprisoned in objects like rings and bottles and will grant three wishes to the fortunate soul that discovers them.

Lamassu: Mesopotamian

The lamassu is a celestial being. Lamassu have wings, a human head, a human body and the horns and ears of a bull. They are known to protect the homes of common Babylonian people.

Leprechaun: Irish

The leprechaun is a miniature magical being. They are usually described as small men, wearing a green hat and coat, with a thick beard. Leprechauns are mischievous and use rainbows to hide their pots of gold.

Manticore: Persian/Greek

The manticore has wings, the head and body of a lion and the tail of a scorpion. The manticore is a very good hunter and eat its prey entirely, bones and all. But it's scared of elephants.

Medusa: Greek

Medusa is a human female with living, venomous snakes on her head instead of hair. Those who gaze into her eyes will turn to stone. Medusa is also a great archer and can hit any target, even if it is moving.

Minotaur: Greek

The minotaur is a mythical creature portrayed with the head and tail of a bull and the body of a man. The minotaur lives at the center of a great labyrinth.

Ogres: European

Ogres are very large, tall and strong creatures with an odd shaped head. They love to eat lots of foods, including animals and people, with naughty people being their favorite.

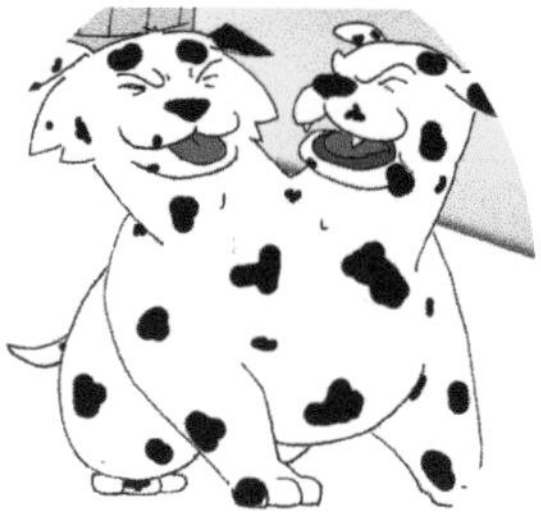

Orthus: Greek

Orthus is a two-headed dog that is owned by a three-headed giant. Orthus guards his master's herd of red cattle.

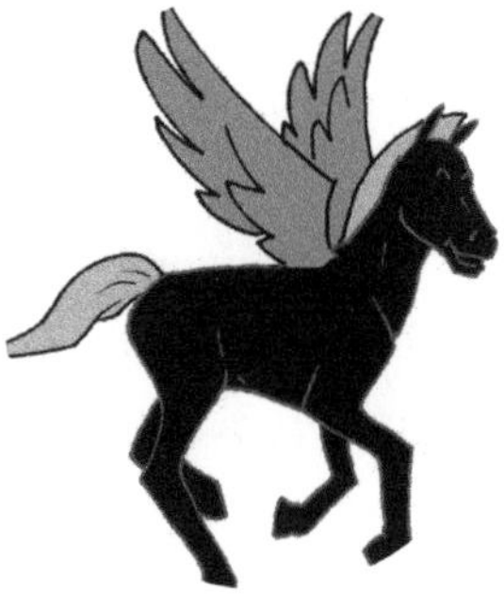

Pegasus: Greek/Roman

Pegasus is a mythical, winged divine horse who helps the heroes Bellerophon and Perseus on their quests.

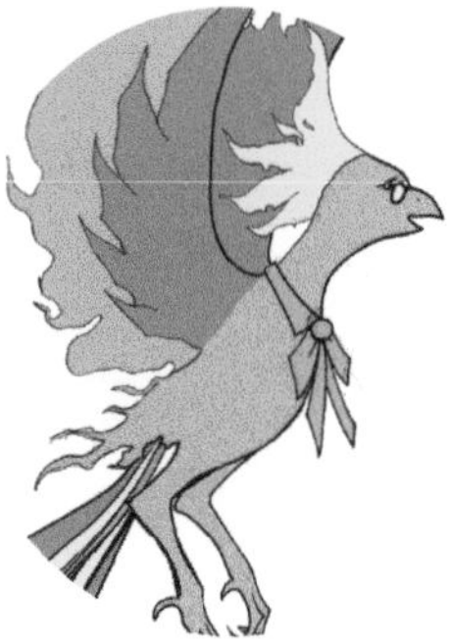

Phoenix: Egyptian/European/Asian

A phoenix is a large, firey eagle and is associated with fire and the sun. A phoenix obtains new life by rising from the ashes of its predecessor. The tears of the phoenix have the ability to heal any wound or infection.

Pixies: British

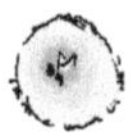

Pixies are said to be friendly for the most part. Pixies have a joyful or happy spirit. But they are also known for their mischief.

Quetzalcoatl: Aztec

Quetzalcoatl is a feathered, flying serpent (much like a dragon) who is a boundary-maker between earth and sky. Quetzalcoatl symbolizes learning and knowledge.

Salamander: European

The salamander looks like a typical salamander in shape with a lizard-like form but much larger. It has the ability to use fire. Ancient salamanders were believed to teach ancient humans how to use fire.

Spriggan: Cornish

Spriggans are tree spirits that have enormous strength. They love treasure and fairies use them as bodyguards.

Thunderbird: North American

The thunderbird is a legendary creature in the history and culture of certain North American indigenous peoples'. It is considered a supernatural being of power and strength. The thunderbird throws lightning and controls the rain and hail. They are also used to punish humans who break moral rules.

Publisher's Cataloging-in-Publication data
Ruby, Jason, 1983–
Griffin's First Day of School/ Jason Ruby; illustrations by Tony Lopez.
48 p.
Includes glossary.
ISBN 978-1-953818-50-8
1. Animals, Mythical—Imaginary Creatures. 2. Imaginary Creatures—Animals, Mythical. I. Ruby, Jason. 1983–. II. Title.
PZ8.1R839 GR 2020

This is a Future Publishing House Publication
Baltimore, Maryland.
ISBN: 978-1-953818-50-8
Illustrations by Tony Lopez

Future Publishing House
KID LIT

CPSIA information can be obtained
at www.ICGtesting.com
Printed in the USA
JSHW012239120421
13507JS00002B/45